Time Travelers **2**

Sherwood Forest
Goes to Pieces

BILL CONDON

Illustrated by Geoff Hocking

Triple3Play

sundance
A Haights Cross Communications Company

Published by
Sundance Publishing
P.O. Box 1326
234 Taylor Street
Littleton, MA 01460
800-343-8204

First published 2001 as Supa Dazzlers by
Pearson Education Australia Pty Limited
95 Coventry Street
South Melbourne 3205 Australia
Exclusive United States Distribution: Sundance Publishing

ISBN 0-7608-6179-X

Printed in Canada

Contents

For Sean, Karen, and Georgia Peters

Chapter 1

Another Adventure

"Where would you like to go?" asked Dad. "Any time, any place. In the past, in the future. You name it, Kendra. We'll hop into the trusty time machine and be there in a blink. But first—have you finished your homework?"

"Yes, Dad. It's all done."

"Good. So where will it be?"

It was great to have a dad who was an inventor. And it was fun the last time Kendra and he went for a ride in the time machine. They had landed in the middle of a jungle.

And now they were about to zoom off on another adventure. There were so many excellent places to choose from!

Kendra knew just where she wanted to go.

"Let's go to Sherwood Forest, Dad."

His eyebrows rose. "You mean, you want to meet . . ."

"Yes. My hero, Robin Hood!"

"Good choice!" said Dad with a big grin. "He's my hero, too. When I was young, I loved to read about Robin and his band of merry men."

"Don't forget Maid Marian," said Kendra. "She was pretty cool, too."

"Oh, yes," he replied. "I can hardly wait to shake her hand. Let's go!"

Chapter 2

The Wrong Turn

They entered the tall, shiny box that was the time machine. This was a very modern time machine. With a flick of a switch, the floor would open, revealing a lab. It was there, with Kendra's help, that Dad created his great inventions. One of these was the world's first flying truck. It was a great idea, but it had a few problems.

Dad also had invented a special grass that could be grown on a bald person's head. The only trouble was that it had to be mowed twice a day.

Since their first trip, Dad had added a very small room to the time machine. The room had a state-of-the-art toilet. Instead of pushing a handle or a button to flush the toilet, you just whistled!

They put on their safety helmets and fastened their seat belts. Then Dad hit the power button.

The time machine groaned into life. It made grumbling, rumbling sounds—like a whole herd of snoring hippos!

Kendra started to worry. "I think it's broken, Dad," she said. "It might even be getting ready to explode!"

Before he could reply, the machine began to rattle. Then it spun faster and faster.

There were flashing lights of pink, yellow, blue, red, and white. There were loud echoes and tiny whispers.

They were in darkness. They were in bright light. They were flying. They were diving. They were screaming!

Then the time machine bounced six times and landed. (Dad had changed things so it no longer hovered above the ground.)

The numbers on the screen telling them what year they were in flashed wildly.

"Are we in the right place?" Kendra asked.

Dad opened the hatch and peered out at the rocky landscape. "It doesn't look like Sherwood Forest," he admitted. "But it must be, because I *never* make mistakes."

All of a sudden, they heard a mighty thump that shook the ground. And another. And another. Looking up, they saw a T-rex standing directly above them!

"Oops," said Dad. "We took a wrong turn."

Chapter 3

In Sherwood Forest

Dad slammed the hatch just as the dinosaur's mouth closed on the machine. Kendra hit the FORWARD button. Suddenly the dinosaur's mouth was empty.

WHOOSH! Once again, Dad and Kendra were zooming through time and space. When they touched down next, they were in the year 1377.

Kendra saw that they were in the middle of some woods. She said with a smile, "Now, this looks more like Sherwood Forest."

But her smile changed to a frown when she noticed large signs hanging from the trees. The signs said:

GO AWAY

YOU'RE NOT WELCOME HERE

WARNING! DANGER AHEAD

And the largest sign of all said:

DON'T EVEN THINK ABOUT ENTERING SHERWOOD FOREST! IF YOU TRY TO, ROBIN HOOD AND HIS ROTTEN RASCALS WILL FEED YOUR GIZZARDS TO THE LIZARDS!

"Robin Hood and his rotten rascals?" said Kendra. "What happened to his merry men?"

Dad, who was always upbeat, replied, "Don't worry. They're probably just having a bad day. Let's go cheer them up."

"I've got a better idea," Kendra said. "Let's go somewhere that's safer—like back home. I *need* my gizzard, Dad."

"Nonsense, Kendra. You're not going to let a few signs scare you off, are you?"

"There's more than just signs. Look closely at the trees," Kendra whispered.

Dad focused his binoculars on the trees. He saw that they were full of people. Robin Hood and his band!

"Yoo-hoo!" Dad called. "We see you!"

The forest erupted with the roar of angry voices. The people jumped down from the trees. They rushed toward Dad and Kendra, screaming one sound.

"AARRGGHH!"

Chapter 4

Bobby Hood

The time travelers raced back toward their machine. As they ran, Kendra glanced over her shoulder and saw that the angry group had stopped. She also noticed that they didn't have any weapons. And then she noticed that they didn't look very scary at all.

"Wait!" she told Dad. "Something tells me they're bluffing."

"How can you be sure?" he asked.

"Just do as I do. OK?"

"OK, Kendra."

Flapping their arms up and down like mad
chickens, Kendra and Dad ran toward Robin
and his band yelling, "**BOO!**"

Looks of fear appeared on the faces of
Robin and his rotten rascals. Then they
turned around and ran for their lives.

Dad took out his newest invention—a skywriting rocket. He pushed a few buttons to get it ready. Then he aimed the rocket at a large cloud and fired. The cloud exploded into tiny pieces that formed this message.

DON'T RUN AWAY. WE WON'T HURT YOU. WE PROMISE.

One by one, Robin and the others stopped running as they saw the message. A large man slowly walked back to Kendra and Dad. He was wearing baggy shorts. His coat barely reached around his middle.

"This isn't one of Prince John's sneaky tricks, is it?" the man asked.

"No way!" Kendra answered. "We're from the future, and we're very friendly. We'd like to help you if we can."

"Oh, yes!" added Dad.

"Oh, that's different," stated the man. "Pull up a log, sit down, and make yourselves at home."

He called the others over. "You can relax," he said. "They're only visitors from the future."

With a firm handshake, the man welcomed Dad and Kendra to Sherwood Forest.

"My name's Robin Hood," he told them, "but my friends call me Bobby."

We're from the future!

Chapter 5

The Best Band

"Please understand," said Bobby, "that we're not really rotten rascals."

"We just put up those signs to scare Prince John's soldiers away," explained a woman. She introduced herself as Wilma Scarlet.

"We knew that," said Dad. "Believe it or not, we know all about you. You're all bold and great fighters."

Kendra patted Bobby on the back. "And you," she said, "are the best swordsman and finest archer in all of England!"

Bobby blushed, as the others roared with laughter. "That's very nice of you. But I've never used a sword, except to open letters."

"None of us have," confessed Wilma.

"And we wouldn't know one end of an arrow from the other," continued Bobby.

Kendra couldn't hide her disbelief. "You're joking," she said. "I've even seen a movie about you. You're a legend!"

"I've never heard of a movie before," replied Bobby. "Has that got something to do with a cow?"

"No! I'm trying to tell you that you *can* sword fight. And you *can* use a bow and arrow!" said Kendra.

"I don't think so," said Bobby, with a shake of his head. "There's only one thing that any of us are good at."

"What's that?" Kendra asked.

All of their lives, Dad and Kendra had read stories about Robin Hood's merry band. Now they found out that was exactly what they were—a band!

Friar Tuckshop played the drums. Little Johnny played the bagpipes. Wilma Scarlet played the fiddle, and Maid Marian played the flute. And her sisters, Maid Mary Lou and Maid Cranky, strummed the banjo.

There was also a small choir. It consisted of Bobby's wife, Robina Hood, and his parents, Mother Hood and Father Hood.

"And I'm their leader," said Bobby proudly. "We're the best band in the land!"

TAP TAP

Chapter 6

Terrible Tunes

"Let's give our guests a foot-tapping tune," Bobby said. "One, two, three . . . hit it!"

Strange sounds blared out of the band's instruments. The fiddle screeched like a cat caught in a door. The flute whistled like a sick crow. The bagpipes squawked like baby vultures. The drums clanged like garbage cans. And the banjos sounded like two frogs learning how to kiss!

And Bobby conducted the band as if he were standing on an ant hill and ants were crawling up his legs!

Bobby winked at Kendra and Dad. "I bet you think that it can't get any better than this," he said. "But just wait until you hear our choir sing."

Robina Hood, Mother Hood, and Father Hood stepped forward. And this is what they sang:

Bobby Hood, Bobby Hood,
and his swinging band.
Bobby Hood, Bobby Hood,
musical and grand.
Hitting the notes, just like he should—
Bobby Hood, Bobby Hood, Bobby Hood!

They used more keys than a locksmith—and every one was different! They were too low and too slow, and Kendra and Dad could hardly believe their ears.

"Well?" asked Bobby. "What do you think about that?"

"Very interesting," Kendra said. "I've never heard music like that before. It's hard to find the words to describe it."

Bobby shook her hand until it almost fell off.

"And what did *you* think of our music, kind sir?" he asked Dad.

Dad strained his brain trying to come up with something nice to say. But, in the end, this was the best that he could do.

"Don't take this wrong, Bobby, but your music is awful. It's bad. It's terrible. Oh, and I almost forgot—it stinks!"

Chapter 7

Dad Finds the Answer

Bobby stumbled backward, as if he'd been shoved by King Kong.

"Rats!" he cried. "That's the worst news I've ever heard!"

"I always knew the band was bad," Father Hood whispered to Dad. "But our singing was good . . . wasn't it?"

Shaking his head sadly, Dad replied, "No. It was awful, too."

"Oh dear!" howled Father Hood. "The pain, the pain!"

Just then a lookout yelled from the treetops. "Horses are coming! It's the wicked Prince John and his evil soldiers!"

"How can you tell?" Bobby yelled back.

"They're all wearing black hats."

"Uh-oh!" Bobby said. "Prince John's always chasing us. He goes crazy when he hears our music. It really makes him angry. I thought that he just had bad taste. But now I know that he was right all along."

"We have to run away," cried Maid Cranky. "If the Prince catches us, he's promised to make us eat our instruments!"

"I love my drums," said Friar Tuckshop, "but not that much!"

"Never fear," Dad said. "Kendra and I are inventors. We'll cook up something to turn you into the best band in the whole world!"

By the time Dad and Kendra got back to the time machine, Dad had come up with a wonderful idea.

"A giant, soundproof bubble! That's the answer!" he exclaimed. "Bobby and the band can put on a concert for Prince John. They can play their music from *inside* the bubble."

"But no one will be able to hear them," said Kendra.

"My plan exactly! While Bobby and the band are playing their music, we'll play great music on a CD. Prince John will think it's coming from them. He'll love it!"

"You're a genius, Dad."

"Yes, I know," he said. "Now, let's begin!"

Chapter 8

The Bubble Bursts

In no time at all, Kendra found some instructions on the Internet for making a giant, soundproof bubble.

Working together, Kendra and Dad poured the ingredients into a bowl. Then they cooked it in the microwave for ten seconds. And just like magic, a sticky, foaming, bubbling mass appeared.

"Now all we need is a special mixture of gas to blow up the stuff," said Dad. "It will make the biggest and best soundproof bubble anyone has ever seen!"

The band members took their place as Dad prepared the gas.

"Are you sure this is safe?" Bobby asked nervously.

"Trust me," said Dad. "I'm *never* wrong."

All of a sudden, Kendra started to worry about their plan. "Maybe this isn't such a good idea after all, Dad," she said.

"Nonsense, Kendra! What could possibly go wrong?"

They would soon find out.

The bubble worked perfectly . . . at first. Within seconds it completely enclosed the band. Dad and Kendra couldn't hear a single note when the band played. But the bubble kept getting bigger and bigger and bigger, until it was huge!

"I hope you didn't put in too much gas," said Kendra.

"Of course not," replied Dad. "You know that I *never* make . . ."

Before he could finish his sentence, the bubble lifted off the ground. It carried the band up higher and higher.

"Oops!" said Dad. "I think we have a little problem."

He and Kendra were too busy watching the bubble to notice the approaching riders. When they heard a man's voice, they realized that some soldiers had arrived.

"Greetings!" the man said. "I am Prince John. Have you seen that evil Bobby Hood and his musical band?"

Kendra and Dad looked up at the sky.

salutations!

Just as Prince John looked up, a flock of birds crashed into the bubble. One bird poked a hole in the bubble. It burst, and Bobby and the band tumbled out of the sky. They landed in a nearby lake.

When they made it to shore, Prince John was waiting.

"At last I've got you!" he snarled.

Chapter 9

Prince John's Surprise

Prince John drew his sword (he was a fine artist) as he waited for the soldiers to bring his real sword.

"Strike me if you must," said Bobby. "But please spare my family and friends."

"Do you still play music?" asked the Prince.

"Yes, of course," answered Bobby.

"Then we must punish you! I can't stand hearing your music!" cried the Prince.

Dad rushed forward holding a CD headset that he always carried with him.

"Put this on when you listen to them play," he told the Prince. "I promise that you'll like what you hear."

Following Dad's instructions, the band gathered up their instruments, tipped the water out of them, and began to play. At the same time, Kendra turned on the CD player. Beautiful music poured into Prince John's ears. He heard the very finest of Mozart and the Beatles.

"Ugh! That's horrible stuff!" he growled. "I hate it! It's giving me a headache!"

He tossed the headset onto the ground and stomped on it.

"But Prince John, it's very good music," Dad said meekly.

"Bah! Humbug! It's rotten!" replied the Prince, and he stomped on the headset again.

"What kind of music *do* you like?" asked Kendra.

Prince John pointed at Bobby and the band. "The kind they play, of course! That's why I dislike them all so much. They're all so good and clever. Their music is so lovely and tender that it makes me cry!"

"Yes!" Bobby shouted. "I knew it! We *are* good!"

"Hurray for Prince John!" cheered the band. "Hurray! Hurray!"

"That's very kind of you," said the Prince, "but still, you all must be punished!"

Chapter 10

Kendra Saves the Day

Always the quiet thinker, Kendra came to the rescue just in the nick of time.

Stepping between Prince John and the band, she said, "There's no need to punish anyone. I have an idea that I'm sure will make everyone happy."

She whispered her plan to Bobby. He slapped her on the back excitedly and told her that it was a terrific idea.

"Just what is this great idea of yours?" demanded Prince John. He looked at Kendra, who smiled at Bobby.

"Well," said Kendra, "Bobby's decided to ask you if you'd like to join his band."

"Wow! Really? Wow! Yippee! Wow!" exclaimed Prince John, jumping up and down in excitement.

"Does that mean yes?" asked Bobby.

"Oh yes! Yes!" the Prince replied. "All of my life I've wanted to be in a band. But no one has ever asked me before. And now I'm going to play in the best band in the whole wide world!"

So Prince John became a member of Bobby Hood's Sherwood Swinging Band.

He played the harp so badly that it sounded like he was plucking feathers from live chickens. But that hardly mattered in Bobby's band because they were all *very, very* bad.

Kendra and Dad were preparing to leave when they noticed one of Prince John's soldiers writing in a notebook.

Kendra approached him curiously and said, "May I ask what you're doing?"

"I write stories," he replied. "I've decided to write one about Prince John and Bobby. But I'll change it a little. All of that music stuff is boring. In my story, Bobby will be a great archer and a swordsman. The readers love that stuff."

Dad and Kendra smiled.

"Here's another idea for you," said Kendra. "Put in something about Bobby stealing from the rich and giving to the poor."

"Hey! What a great idea. I like it!" said the soldier. "That's really good stuff! That's just what I'll do. Thanks a lot!"

As Dad and Kendra climbed back into the time machine, they could hear awful sounds coming from the forest. And then an equally awful choir began to sing . . .

Bobby Hood, Bobby Hood,
and his swinging band.
Bobby Hood, Bobby Hood,
musical and grand.
Hitting the notes, just like he should—
Bobby Hood, Bobby Hood, Bobby Hood!

About the Author

Bill Condon

Bill Condon is a typical writer—fabulously wealthy, genius IQ, incredibly handsome, and, of course, tremendously humble.

Unfortunately, he suffers from really scary nightmares. Why, just last week he dreamed that he was being sawed into pieces by a chain saw.

It was his own fault . . . he was sleeping like a log!

About the Illustrator

Geoff Hocking

Geoff Hocking started illustrating books for children during the 1970s, when he and his wife, Christine, lived and worked in London.

Since then he has illustrated dozens of books, written some, painted pictures, built a house of mud, spent too much money on foreign cars, and taught design and illustration to hundreds of people.

He and Christine have three children. One is a fashion designer, one is a graphic designer, and one is a preteen who does crazy drawings and worries about losing his hair.